FREMONT PUBLIC LIBRARY

3 3090 00250 4290

11-04

D1365172

Flynn Flies High

By Hilary Robinson

Illustrated by Tim Archbold

Special thanks to our advisers for their expertise:

Adria F. Klein, Ph.D.
Professor Emeritus, California State University
San Bernardino, California

Susan Kesselring, M.A.
Literacy Educator
Rosemount-Apple Valley-Eagan (Minnesota) School District

WITHDRAWN

PICTURE WINDOW BOOKS
Minneapolis, Minnesota

Fremont Public Library
1170 N. Midlothian Road
Mundelein, IL 60060

Levels for *Read-it!* Readers

- Familiar topics
- Frequently used words
- Repeating patterns

- New ideas
- Larger vocabulary
- Variety of language structures

- Challenges in ideas
- Expanded vocabulary
- Wide variety of sentences

- More complex ideas
- Extended vocabulary range
- Expanded language structures

A Note to Parents and Caregivers:

Read-it! Readers are for children who are just starting on the amazing road to reading. These beautiful books support both the acquisition of reading skills and the love of books.

The RED LEVEL presents familiar topics using common words and repeating sentence patterns.

The BLUE LEVEL presents new ideas using a larger vocabulary and varied sentence structure.

The YELLOW LEVEL presents more challenging ideas, a broad vocabulary, and wide variety in sentence structure.

The GREEN LEVEL presents more complex ideas, an extended vocabulary range, and expanded language structures.

When sharing a book with your child, read in short stretches, pausing often to talk about the pictures. Have your child turn the pages and point to the pictures and familiar words. And be sure to reread favorite stories or parts of stories.

There is no right or wrong way to share books with children. Find time to read with your child, and pass on the legacy of literacy.

Adria F. Klein, Ph.D.
Professor Emeritus
California State University
San Bernardino, California

First American edition published in 2005 by
Picture Window Books
5115 Excelsior Boulevard
Suite 232
Minneapolis, MN 55416
877-845-8392
www.picturewindowbooks.com

First published in Great Britain by Franklin Watts, 96 Leonard Street,
London, EC2A 4XD

Text © Hilary Robinson 2003
Illustration © Tim Archbold 2003

All rights reserved. No part of this book may be reproduced without written permission
from the publisher. The publisher takes no responsibility for the use of any of the materials
or methods described in this book, nor for the products thereof.

Printed in the United States of America.

Library of Congress Cataloging-in-Publication Data
Robinson, Hilary, 1962-
Flynn flies high / by Hilary Robinson ; illustrated by Tim Archbold.
p. cm. — (Read-it! readers)
Summary: A boy befriends a classmate who others ridicule and exclude, right up until the
day they all visit the circus.
ISBN 1-4048-0563-X (hardcover)
[1. Teasing—Fiction. 2. Aerialists—Fiction.] I. Archbold, Tim, ill. II. Title. III. Series.
PZ7.R566175Fl 2004
[E]—dc22   2004007619

No one at school wanted to be
Flynn's friend—except Jack.

Flynn didn't come to school every day. He didn't wear the right clothes or do very well in class.

Some children talked behind his
back and wouldn't sit next
to him.

Flynn was good at some things.

He could do back flips

and cartwheels.

8

But because he couldn't play
soccer, no one wanted him
on their team—except Jack.

Then Flynn was absent from school one day, and the day after that, and the day after that.

In fact, he was away for weeks.
And Jack was the only person
who noticed.

Then, during soccer practice, everyone watched as a traveling circus went past.

They were all quiet until someone shouted, "Look! There's Flynn! And look—his house has wheels!"

And everyone laughed—

except Jack.

The other children soon forgot
about Flynn. But one day, heavy rain
made the soccer field so wet that no
one could practice.

They were all moaning when
someone joked that Flynn's house
would be stuck in the mud. And
everyone laughed—except Jack.

Then someone suggested going
to the circus instead.
So off they went!

Everyone got excited when the ringmaster cried, "Welcome, everyone! Welcome to our show!

To help get us off to a swinging start, please give a big welcome to Flynn on the Flying Trapeze!"

For once, no one said a word.

After a dazzling display of
daring dives, twists and turns,

and swings through hoops high,
high above the crowd,
Flynn landed and bowed.

The crowd cheered and yelled for
more. The ringmaster said, "Flynn!
Flynn! Listen to that roar!

You must have lots of your friends
out there. Why don't you invite
them to join you in the ring?"

Flynn simply smiled and said, "Yes, I've got lots of good friends, but I didn't have any at school before—

except Jack!"

Levels for *Read-it!* Readers

Read-it! Readers help children practice early reading
skills with brightly illustrated stories.

Red Level: Familiar topics with frequently used words and
repeating patterns.

I Am in Charge of Me by Dana Meachen Rau
Let's Share by Dana Meachen Rau

Blue Level: New ideas with a larger vocabulary and a variety
of language structures.

At the Beach by Patricia M. Stockland
The Playground Snake by Brian Moses

Yellow Level: Challenging ideas with an expanded vocabulary
and a wide variety of sentences.

Flynn Flies High by Hilary Robinson
Marvin, the Blue Pig by Karen Wallace
Moo! by Penny Dolan
Pippin's Big Jump by Hilary Robinson
The Queen's Dragon by Anne Cassidy
Sounds Like Fun by Dana Meachen Rau
Tired of Waiting by Dana Meachen Rau
Whose Birthday Is It? by Sherryl Clark

Green Level: More complex ideas with an extended vocabulary
range and expanded language structures.

Clever Cat by Karen Wallace
Flora McQuack by Penny Dolan
Izzie's Idea by Jillian Powell
Naughty Nancy by Anne Cassidy
The Princess and the Frog by Margaret Nash
The Roly-Poly Rice Ball by Penny Dolan
Run! by Sue Ferraby
Sausages! by Anne Adeney
Stickers, Shells, and Snow Globes by Dana Meachen Rau
The Truth About Hansel and Gretel by Karina Law
Willie the Whale by Joy Oades

A complete list of *Read-it!* Readers is available on our Web site:
www.picturewindowbooks.com

18.60